Lunch With A Blue Kitty

Lunch With A Blue Kitty

written & illustrated by
Scarlett Montana

PALMETTO
PUBLISHING
Charleston, SC
www.PalmettoPublishing.com

Copyright © 2024 by Scarlett Montana

All rights reserved
No portion of this book may be reproduced, stored in a retrieval system, or transmitted in any form by any means—electronic, mechanical, photocopy, recording, or other—except for brief quotations in printed reviews, without prior permission of the author.

First Edition

Hardcover ISBN: 979-8-8229-4913-3
Paperback ISBN: 979-8-8229-4914-0

*Dedicated to those
who rescue
and provide sanctuary*

Once upon a warm spring day,
I found lunchtime calling
and spied a café.

I saw delightful tables under the sun,
so I inquired within
about a table for one.

"But of course, Mademoiselle,
we would love for you to dine.
But a table for one
will take a bit of time."

"Unless, Mademoiselle,
you're so intent on quick fare,
that you might consider dining
with the gentlemen over there."

The maître d' pointed at a table
perfect for two
where alone sat a kitty,
the color of blue.

I pondered for a moment
over the table to share.
*Lunch with a blue kitty
must certainly be rare.*

"Pardon me, Monsieur,
but would you be so kind
as to welcome this fine lady
for tea and to dine?"

The gracious kitty welcomed me
with a smile and a purr.
I took my seat across the table
from this feline with blue fur.

We ate hors d'oeuvres, sandwiches
and sipped a spot of tea.
I had pastries for dessert
as he recited poetry.

As we finished our meal,
I could not help but say,
"What in the world
is a blue kitty doing in a café?"

"I once had a family.
But they left me behind.
They moved far away
and I'm still not sure why."

This kitty is so brave.
As he spoke, I shed a tear.
He was left all alone,
confused, hungry and scared.

"I was alone for a while,
'til I came to this café.
They said, 'Stay away from the fish tank
and you're welcome to stay.'"

"They keep me company and pet me,
so I watch for burglars and mice.
They feed me every morning
and leave a bed for me at night."

"So, Madame, you ask why I sit
in a café in the city?
It's in hopes of telling good people like you
what it's like to be a blue kitty."

"We are living beings,
with feelings just like you.
We're here to make you happy
but it's important we're happy too."

"Many of you like us
and have taken us as pets.
We love having families
and don't mind visits to the vet."

"We need fresh water and fresh food."

"We need shelter from cold and from heat."

"We love to play and cuddle with you, and we like an occasional treat."

"For those who do not like us,
when you see us, please don't fuss.
There is no need to be cruel,
throw rocks at us or cuss."

"We are all creatures of this earth
and this I know for sure; we must learn
to treat each other with kindness whether
we have skin or feathers or fur."

I thanked the blue kitty for this finest
of hours. We embraced and I bid him farewell.
I promised that I would never forget him
and his story I will surely tell.

The Beginning